SHADOW
SQUADRON

DRAGON
TEETH

raintree
a Capstone company — publishers for children

SHADOW
SQUADRON

DRAGON TEETH

WRITTEN BY
CARL BOWEN

ILLUSTRATED BY
WILSON TORTOSA

AND
BENNY FUENTES

COVER ART BY
MARC LEE

AUTHORIZING

2012.241

Raintree is an imprint of Capstone Global Library
Limited, a company incorporated in England and
Wales having its registered office at 7 Pilgrim
Street, London, EC4V 6LB – Registered company
number: 6695582

www.raintree.co.uk
myorders@raintree.co.uk

First published by Stone Arch Books © 2015
First published in the United Kingdom in 2015

ISBN: 978-1-4747-0542-4 (paperback)
ISBN: 978-1-4747-0547-9 (eBook PDF)

British Library Cataloguing in Publication Data

A full catalogue record for this book is available
from the British Library.

Printed in China

CONTENTS

1316.981

2012.101

SHADOW SQUADRON DOSSIER

CROSS, RYAN

RANK: Lieutenant Commander
BRANCH: Navy SEAL
PSYCH PROFILE: Cross is the team leader of Shadow Squadron. Control oriented and loyal, Cross insisted on hand-picking each member of his squad.

PHOTO NOT
AVAILABLE

PAXTON, ADAM

RANK: Sergeant First Class
BRANCH: Army (Green Beret)
PSYCH PROFILE: Paxton has a knack for filling the role most needed in any team. His loyalty makes him a born second-in-command.

YAMASHITA, KIMIYO

RANK: Lieutenant
BRANCH: Army Ranger
PSYCH PROFILE: The team's sniper is an expert marksman and a true stoic. It seems his emotions are as steady as his trigger finger.

LANCASTER, MORGAN

RANK: Staff Sergeant
BRANCH: Air Force Combat Control
PSYCH PROFILE: The team's newest member is a tech expert who learns fast and has the ability to adapt to any combat situation.

PHOTO NOT AVAILABLE

JANNATI, ARAM

RANK: Second Lieutenant
BRANCH: Army Ranger
PSYCH PROFILE: Jannati serves as the team's linguist. His sharp eyes serve him well as a spotter, and he's usually paired with Yamashita on overwatch.

PHOTO NOT AVAILABLE

SHEPHERD, MARK

RANK: Lieutenant
BRANCH: Army (Green Beret)
PSYCH PROFILE: The heavy-weapons expert of the group, Shepherd's love of combat borders on unhealthy.

2019.681

MISSION BRIEFING

OPERATION

DRAGON TEETH 010

We've been informed that an ally of a traitor of the CIA (as well as Shadow Squadron) has been located in Iran. His name is Carter Howard, and he's evaded capture by the CIA, so we've been tasked with tracking him down and bringing him in for questioning.

He's currently in deep cover as a terrorist. We're going to have to ambush a meet and greet between his faction and another group to get our hands on him. If we can disrupt the alliance between the two terrorist groups in the process, so be it.

– Lieutenant Commander Ryan Cross

3245.98 ● ● ●

IRAN

PRIMARY OBJECTIVE(S)

- Locate Carter Howard

- Question him

SECONDARY OBJECTIVE(S)

- Destabilize relationship between
  Al-Qaeda and Jundallah

INTEL

DECRYPTING

12345

COM CHATTER

- .50 CAL: type of machine gun round
- CANALPHONE: a radio earpiece that fits inside the ear canal
- OVERWATCH: one small unit that positions itself so it can see the terrain and any incoming threats

3245.98

CHAPTER ONE

FISHING

Green Beret Sergeant Mark Shepherd smirked. "All right, Commander," he said. "Our frenemy is coming."

"Roger that," Lieutenant Commander Ryan Cross replied. His tone was amusement and annoyance in equal parts. If Cross didn't know Shepherd so well, he might've believed the man lying on the ground next to him wasn't taking the operation seriously.

Cross tapped the two-way canalphone nestled in his left ear. "Ready up, people," he said to the rest of his soldiers. "Our target's inbound."

"Right on time," Sergeant First Class Adam Paxton replied over the radio. Paxton, the other Green Beret on Cross's team, was Cross's second-in-command. His fireteam was in position opposite Cross's team. The space between them was about to become a deadly field of fire. "Their buyers are on the way up the other side of the hill."

"How many?" Cross asked.

"One jeep, mounted with a .50 cal," Paxton said. "Three men there. One pick-up truck, packed full. Ten men there, all armed. And one box truck, probably holding the payment. Driver and one passenger in that one. Fifteen soldiers in total, not counting anyone who might be in the back of the truck."

"They brought a whole box truck?" Shepherd muttered. "That's a lot of drugs."

Cross looked into the distance, away from the hillside Paxton's fire team had covered. A road that barely qualified as such stretched out across the barren, rugged flats. The desert disappeared into the hazy morning sun. Dust rose in the wake of the approaching vehicles.

Cross tapped his canalphone once more. "Overwatch, can you make out exact numbers coming with our–"

"Frenemy?" Shepherd interrupted. "You can say it, Commander."

Cross smirked. "Our target," he finished.

Lieutenant Kimiyo Yamashita, an Army Ranger and the team's sniper, was perched 50 metres away on overwatch. He lay prone on a rocky crag that looked like a fang biting up through Earth's crust. "Three tankers, two men each. One panelled van – passenger and a driver. That's all I can see."

"Can you tell which one's our target?" Cross asked.

"Not yet, Commander," Yamashita replied. "I'll call out when I spot him. Just make sure Lancaster's droids don't shoot him."

From Cross's left came a small, annoyed groan from Staff Sergeant Morgan Lancaster. Although she had been on the team for months, helped with dozens of missions, and even saved Cross's life, he still thought of her as the new tech expert. Perhaps that would change when she'd been on the team longer than the soldier she'd replaced.

"I wish he wouldn't call them that," Lancaster said. "It's not like they're robots. They're just tools."

Wickedly effective tools, Cross reflected.

The hardware in question was a pair of remotely operated sniper rifles. They were arranged opposite Yamashita. The two weapons were positioned in a triangle with Yamashita being the third point of it. Both of the devices sat in camo nests atop heavy-duty tripods. They could move forty-five degrees up, down, left or right – all with minimal shaking and in near silence. Atop each rifle sat a $10,000 scope with a laser range-finder, a night-vision system, a tiny Wi-Fi server, a fibre-optic camera and many other advancements.

Images from the scopes were transmitted to a tablet computer on the ground in front of Yamashita. With one finger, he could mark and eliminate targets. The guns' tripods could track the marked, moving targets and fire with astonishing accuracy.

The rifles could also be operated via the tactical datapads in the bracers on the other soldiers' left forearms, but only if Yamashita approved it on the tablet in front of him. For now, the team could bring up a feed from the guns' cameras and see what they saw, which was extremely useful when multiple positions were needed in the field.

The weapons, which Lancaster preferred be called autoguns, had been the combat controller's latest contribution to the team's weaponry. (The datapad bracers had been her idea as well.) Cross had been sceptical of the technology, as had Yamashita. But Lancaster had demonstrated its effectiveness on stationary and moving targets at the range where the weapons had been developed, which quickly changed their minds.

This mission was the first one in which they would actually use the autoguns. Cross wanted to make sure the technology was reliable in the field. To that end, he'd given Yamashita strict orders not to give anyone else on the team access to the systems unless necessary – and then only to Cross himself.

Concerns about the autoguns aside, Cross was pleased to have extra firepower. He had only six soldiers with him, and the enemy numbered at least twenty-three. Three-to-one odds against was a bad ratio for an attacking force, even with the element of surprise and one as well-trained as Shadow Squadron.

None of the soldiers in the two groups that were about to meet had any idea they were moving into Cross's team's sights. Despite that fact, these soldiers were still dangerous, battle-hardened men. They were criminals and killers and self-proclaimed holy warriors. Once the initial shock wore off from the surprise assault, they would put up a hard fight. And when that happened, the more barrels Cross could point at the bad guys, the better. And if some of those barrels never missed, better still.

"Commander, we've got about one minute," Paxton said through the canalphones.

"Got it," Cross replied. He tapped his canalphone. "Sixty seconds, people. Remember, we need our target alive. Let's keep the hard stuff away from the van, as it's his likely location. I don't want any accidents."

"What about the box truck, Sir?" Second Lieutenant Aram Jannati asked over the comm channel.

"Consider it a secondary target," Cross said after a slight hesitation. "But it's not a priority. I'll decide what we do with it after the smoke clears. Our goal is to neutralize the hostiles and secure the target."

"Not to knock the plan, Sir," the team's medic, Hospital Corpsman Second Class Kyle Williams said. "But how do we stop the target getting taken out in the crossfire down there?"

"His psych profile indicates he's not going to stick around once things get dangerous," Cross said. "He's not going to put himself in a position where he has to stand and fight. He's going to take cover and hide and try to get away without anyone seeing him."

"Understood, Sir," Williams said.

"Eyes on the target," Yamashita reported a moment later. "Passenger seat of the van. White shirt, brown scarf, desert-camo jacket. Sending the picture now."

BZZZT.

The datapad on Cross's left forearm gave the slightest vibration. He tapped it to bring it to life. On it was a picture of a man in his late thirties. It was definitely their target, though the image was slightly grainy having been taken through the dusty windscreen of the van. A sharp dot of red light lay between his eyes.

"Did you take this picture with one of my autoguns?" Lancaster whispered through her teeth. Cross heard Shepherd snort laughter on the other side of him.

"No comment," Yamashita said dryly.

"That's him," Cross confirmed. "Make sure nobody shoots him. Not us, not them."

"Everybody fire selectively," Paxton added. "The longer they take to work out our location, the better."

The box truck pulled up from one direction and the three tankers from the other.

"All right, they're almost in position," Cross said. "Get ready."

* * *

Seventy-two hours earlier…

For once, Cross was the last one to the briefing room. Six pairs of eyes looked up from smartphones as he sat down at the long table. Like other mornings, Paxton brought Cross a cup of coffee. A little wisp of steam rose from the hole in its plastic lid.

Cross accepted the coffee, nodded his thanks, and took a sip. "Morning," he said. "Before anybody asks, still no word from Congress."

Grumbling filled the room. For weeks, Cross had been sending requests up through the chain of command for a new soldier to fill his team's most recent vacancy. The approval process was slow going, due to the congressman at the head of the budgeting committee. The Honourable James Barron was upset with the way Cross had handled an earlier mission in Mali some months ago. Ever since then, Senator Barron had been looking for ways to undermine and annoy him – such as delaying approval for staff replacements.

Despite being short one soldier, Cross's team was

as formidable as they came. Shadow Squadron was a top-secret special missions unit assembled by the United States' Joint Special Operations Command. Its members were elite soldiers from all branches of the military. The team had travelled all over the world rooting out terrorist threats, hunting international criminals, rescuing hostages, defending foreign leaders, wiping out slavers and even fighting pirates. From one end of the world to the other, the team had showed up wherever the US government had an interest in military intervention but couldn't act openly. The six soldiers who remained under Cross's command had dozens of successful operations under their belts. The failure to replace one of their own was a hardship, but they had faced worse and still found success.

"While we wait," Cross continued, "we've got an operation to keep us busy. A fishing expedition in sunny Balochistan."

Cross tapped the screen of a tablet computer inset in the tabletop, bringing it and the projector mounted in the ceiling to life. Behind him, the swords-and-globe emblem of Joint Special Operations Command appeared. He swiped a folder from the datapad on his forearm to the tablet computer. A variety of files were displayed on the screen.

With the right software, Cross could have run the presentation from his datapad or sent the images directly to his soldiers' datapads. Lancaster had pointed this out after almost every briefing since the datapads had been implemented. But Cross didn't want to spend every briefing looking at the tops of his soldiers' heads as they stared down at their forearms.

"This is the fish we're going to catch," he said. Cross enlarged a file photo of a man in his mid-thirties. He had Middle-Eastern features, coarse black hair and a slightly shaggy beard. "He's currently going by the name of Yusuf, but his real name's Carter Howard. He was born and raised in Tennessee. He went to college on an Army ROTC scholarship, put in his mandatory four years in Military Intelligence, and joined the CIA immediately after. He's been kicking around the Special Activities Division for the last ten years under the employ of Special Agent Bradley Upton."

Cross paused. His soldiers nodded knowingly. Bradley Upton had been a long-serving, well-connected CIA operative who'd worked with Shadow Squadron several times. He had also been an immoral con-man taking advantage of the War on Terror to steal money. Upton tried to recruit Cross and cut him in on the action, but that conversation had not played out as the traitor expected. Now Upton was gone, and the CIA had been scrambling to clean up the messes he'd left behind. This time, they reached out to Shadow Squadron. Cross had no problem helping them out with this task – considering Upton had tried to kill him.

"Howard's last legitimate assignment was to infiltrate the Iranian terrorist organization Jundallah and gather intel to help bring it down from within," Cross continued. "He's operating in Balochistan, which is here."

Cross replaced Howard's photo and dossier with a map of the Middle East, centred on Iran's south-eastern border. On the left side of the map was Iran. On the right was Pakistan. Afghanistan was to the north. The Arabian Sea opened to the south. He traced the border region between Iran and Pakistan with his fingertip, highlighting it on the screen behind him.

"Howard has worked his way into a unit that hijacks diesel tankers moving out of Zahedan and smuggles them across the border into Pakistan or Afghanistan. Diesel fuel is about five times more expensive there. They trade the diesel for opium, which Jundallah sells back into Iran for a huge profit."

"So these soldiers of God are just glorified drug dealers?" Yamashita asked.

Cross knew Yamashita well enough to hear the slight agitation in the stoic sniper's voice.

"It funds their terrorist acts," Paxton put in. "Jundallah says it's justified in the name of standing up for Sunni Muslims."

After a popular revolution in 1979, Iran had been taken over by followers of Islam. The leaders of that revolution, and an overwhelming majority of the Muslims in the country, followed the Shia sect of that religion. That meant the Sunnis were comparatively powerless to influence the government. Jundallah wanted to permanently change that at any cost.

"Jundallah 'stands up' for Sunnis by kidnapping and bombing soldiers and civilians," Paxton continued. "Make no mistake, they're a terrorist organization. They also have ties to Al-Qaeda in Afghanistan and Pakistan. This smuggling and drug dealing pays out hugely to both organizations in all three countries."

"And this Carter Howard – Yusuf – guy?" Yamashita asked. "I assume he's lining his own pockets in the process, just like Upton had been."

"So it seems," Cross answered. "He went dark shortly after the investigation into Upton began. His superiors tried to bring him back in for questioning, but he refused. They sent a couple of agents in to aggressively convince him to come home, and both of them disappeared. Now the CIA has a pretty good idea where Howard's going to be, but they want us to be the ones to scoop him up."

"Where's he going to be?" Williams asked.

"Chatter from Pakistan indicates that Howard's group has a deal going down in seventy-two hours with an Al-Qaeda-affiliated cell," Cross said. He tapped a spot on the map. "It'll be here, on the Pakistan border. The CIA wants us to find Howard there, capture him alive and turn him in for questioning."

"And what does Command want us to do?" Shepherd asked. "Not exactly the same thing, I'm thinking."

"No," Cross said. "Command wants us to question Howard before we turn him over – just in case the CIA has second thoughts about letting us question him *after* they do. Command also wants us to do more than just watch as this opium trade goes down. They want us to bust up the deal and eliminate as many of the terrorists as we can. If we do it right, we might be able to drive a wedge between Al-Qaeda and Jundallah in the process."

Paxton added, "And if nothing else, weakening both organizations and messing with their cash flow is a pretty good consolation prize."

Cross nodded. His steely gaze caught Paxton's attention. "As long as we still come away with Carter Howard, that is," Cross said. "I won't tolerate him following in Upton's footsteps."

INTEL

DECRYPTING

12345

COM CHATTER

- M110 RIFLE: semi-automatic sniper rifle
- MORPHINE: powerful pain reliever and sedative
- SUPPRESSING FIRE: gunfire used to keep enemy combatants pinned down behind cover or used to provide cover for one's own troops

3245.98 ● ● ●

CHAPTER TWO

AMBUSHED

1324.014

Both Cross and Paxton's fire teams tensed into silent readiness as the stolen oil tankers arrived. The Pakistani criminal contacts approached from the other direction with their shipment of opium. Their destination was what remained of an abandoned village in the wastelands of Saravan, Iran. The place was so empty and broken down that it looked like no one had lived there for centuries. The Al-Qaeda and Jundallah men knew the place by name and seemed to have no trouble finding it. However, it had taken Shadow Squadron several days to determine its location. They'd arrived mere hours before the exchange was to take place.

The two sets of terrorists brought their vehicles to a halt on opposite sides of a village. The drivers of the oil tankers and the box truck removed the keys and stood behind their respective leaders. Narrowed eyes and clutched firearms made it clear that neither side wholly trusted the other. That fact relieved Cross. His plan relied on the groups' mistrust of one another.

On the Pakistani side, the men in the back of the pick-up truck jumped out and gathered around their leader. The gunner on the jeep kept his weapon trained on the van that had come with the Jundallah tankers. From that side, a number of men just short of those on the Al-Qaeda side emerged from the back and side doors of the van. They milled around its front end. The only one to stay inside was Carter Howard, who remained in the passenger seat, smoking a cigarette.

The apparent leader of the Jundallah cell briefly spoke to his tanker drivers, then began to walk out into the area between the two groups. The Al-Qaeda cell leader began to walk towards the middle of the open expanse. The drivers of the tankers and box truck followed a step behind their respective leaders. The armed men who'd come along for the ride came forward as well, staying several steps behind the drivers in loose clumps of two or three. They all eyed their foreign counterparts like rival packs of dogs.

The two groups met in the middle of the village. The two hard, stone-faced leaders stood glaring at each other. Their AK-47 rifles were clutched across their chests, ready to spring into battle at a moment's notice.

Cross tapped on his canalphone. "Overwatch, it's your call," he said. "Throw the stone when you're ready."

That last comment referenced to a story from Greek mythology. In the tale, a soldier called Jason found himself facing an army of skeletal soldiers that had sprung up from the ground where dragons' teeth had been buried. Rather than allow himself to be surrounded and overwhelmed, Jason hid and threw a stone into the middle of the skeletal soldiers. The stone struck one of them, and the skeletons assumed that one of their own had thrown it. Thus, they turned on each other, tearing one another's limbs off. It was from this story that Cross had taken inspiration for his own plan, casting Yamashita in the role of Jason.

FWIP.

The sniper's first shot took the .50-cal. gunner off the back of the jeep in a sudden jolt. No one heard the shot thanks to the suppressor on Yamashita's M110 rifle.

No one on the Al-Qaeda side of the meeting even realized what had happened. But one of the gunmen on the Jundallah side saw the man fall. He lurched back a step and raised his rifle, calling out for his fellow fighters to watch out.

Yamashita tapped the tablet in front of him. The autoguns' targeting reticle centred over the Al-Qaeda cell leader's chest.

FWIP.

Its silenced shot caught the man square in the chest.

RAT–TAT–TAT–TAT–TAT–TAT–TAT!

He squeezed his AK-47's trigger reflexively as he fell, spraying bullets in a wild arc that caught one of the tanker drivers in the stomach. The pair of them crumpled together.

What the men on the Al-Qaeda side saw was one of the Jundallah gunmen raise his rifle, shout out a challenge, and gun down their leader.

What the men on the Jundallah side saw was the Al-Qaeda leader wildly open fire on them before one of their own shouted a warning and put the Pakistani down with a single shot in the chest.

At that point, the fog of battle descended on them all and chaos broke out.

BANG BANG BANG BANG BANG BANG BANG BANG BANG BANG BANG BANG BANG BANG BANG BANG BANG BANG BANG BANG BANG BANG

Guns came up on both sides. Bullets started flying. The Jundallah leader actually lowered his rifle and tried to shout for everyone to calm down and stop fighting. A second later, bullets from three different Al-Qaeda shooters placed him face down in the dust. No one else was killed in the initial outbreak, but only because everyone on both sides was more concerned with running away to find cover than firing accurately. They ran around and behind and beneath whatever broken bits of wall or tumbled-down roof they thought might shelter them.

WHIRRR-FWIP!
WHIRRR-FWIP!

Yamashita took the opportunity to mark and eliminate two more targets with the autoguns. A shot from his own rifle punched a hole in the engine block of the van Howard was sitting in just as the CIA man had lurched over into the driver's seat and tried to get the vehicle in gear. Instead of starting, a plume of grey smoke billowed up through the bonnet. Howard scrambled out of his seat into the back of the van and took cover, disappearing from Yamashita's view.

The gunfire dropped off as both sides tried to determine each others' positions. Men began scuttling around behind their cover, looking for lines of sight over their enemies' cover, or for lines of retreat back to their vehicles. If both sides had attempted to retreat immediately, they might have survived the conflict. But it seemed neither side had any interest in leaving its respective cargo behind.

Everyone involved understood that gaining control of the battlefield relied on gaining or denying access to the machine gun. Otherwise, the Al-Qaeda and Jundallah fighters would have settled into a stalemate as both sides locked each other down with suppressing fire.

Shadow Squadron took steps to prevent that happening, however. Yamashita took one more shot through each of the autoguns, timing his fire with the terrorists' own fire. A third bullet from his M110 took out an Al-Qaeda fighter who'd climbed up onto the back of an old-fashioned wind tower. The man's rifle tumbled from his lifeless fingers to give a nasty knock on the head to his comrade taking cover directly below him.

As Yamashita and the autoguns reloaded, the sniper set one of them to point at the jeep's machine gun. The other he aimed at the Jundallah side's cover. He managed to pick off one more Iranian terrorist with that gun, as well as one clever Al-Qaeda member wriggling into the opening of the village's irrigation tunnel.

With no one else brave enough to make a break for the machine gun, everyone hunkered down behind their cover.

"Commander, I'm out of targets," Yamashita reported over the comm channel.

"Roger that," Cross replied in a whisper. "We'll see what we can do to flush some out for you."

Amidst the chaos, Cross and Paxton's fire teams had moved up unnoticed on the Al-Qaeda and Jundallah fighters. Cross's fire team was on the Pakistanis' side with the rising sun on their backs.

Paxton's team was directly behind the Jundallah fighters, concealed in a ditch hidden by long shadows. At identical hand gestures from Cross and Paxton, the teams split up and picked their targets. As one, they opened fire from concealment.

FWIP-PING-FWIP! PING-FWIP!

The suppressors on their M4 carbines made it all the more difficult to tell where the shots were coming from.

The result was a fresh wave of chaos. The fighters nearest the ones who'd been shot panicked and abandoned perfectly good cover. Their panic made them actual targets for the very shooters they were hoping to elude, costing lives on both sides. When the shooters rose to fire at their panicked enemies, Yamashita eliminated them in groups of three.

Meanwhile, Cross and Paxton's fire teams kept moving and shooting the targets that Yamashita and the autoguns couldn't see. At no point did the

Jundallah or Al-Qaeda gunmen realize that a third party was working against them both.

This last wave of violence broke the fighting spirit of the few men left alive. The last remaining Jundallah survivor who wasn't Carter Howard simply bolted into the desert, abandoning his comrades and the vehicles.

The five Pakistani survivors were able to drag themselves to the jeep they'd arrived in. One of them died as his comrades were trying to pull him in with them. Yamashita put down another one with his M110 as he put on his seat belt. The driver slammed the jeep into reverse, whipped the vehicle around in a semicircle, then tore off through the desert back towards Pakistan.

Shadow Squadron rose from their positions and secured the field of battle. Only one terrorist was still alive – and in pretty bad shape. The middle-aged man's blood-stained beard twitched as he tried to speak. When Paxton found the man, he nodded at Williams. The medic eased the dying terrorist's passing with a syringe of morphine.

"No targets remain," Yamashita reported.

"Clear," Paxton reported as his fire team gathered back up on their side of the field.

"All clear," Cross confirmed from his side.

With the field secured, all that remained for the team was to collect Carter Howard and call in Shadow Squadron's stealth helicopter, the Wraith.

"Overwatch, is the target still locked down?" Cross asked.

"Sir," Yamashita replied. "I can still see him on the floor of the van."

"Is he armed?" Cross asked.

"I can't tell, but I know I didn't shoot him," the sniper said.

"Fair enough," Cross said. "Gather up the autoguns and reel in."

"Sir," Yamashita said again.

"Fireteam two," Cross said, "join us by the van."

"Sir," Paxton said.

A moment later, he, Jannati and Williams jogged across the field to join Cross, Shepherd and Lancaster. Together, the six of them circled the van with their carbines at the ready, covering any door through which Howard might try to escape. Cross moved to the sliding side door.

KNOCK! KNOCK!

Cross pounded on the door twice with his fist. "Carter Howard," he called. "Get out of the van with your hands behind your head."

"*Goh khordi*," Cross heard Howard mutter from within. Then, in English tinged with a Southern drawl, Howard said, "Okay, take it easy out there. I don't want any trouble. Do you want to open the door, or shall I?"

"Do not try my patience," Cross growled.

"All right then. Just didn't want there to be any confusion. Give me a sec." The van rocked a little as Howard got up off the floor and moved over to the

side door. "Okay, now before I open this door, just remember: I'm one of the good guys."

Cross opened his mouth to bark something unpleasant, but Howard was already opening the door. The man sat empty-handed between the seats. His mouth opened to say something, but when he saw Cross, his eyes narrowed and his mouth closed. He even gave an exaggerated flinch of confusion.

"Hold on," he said. "I know you. You're Ryan Cross."

INTEL

DECRYPTING

12345

COM CHATTER

- DOSSIER: file on a subject or person intended to be used to inform soldiers
- MANHATTAN PROJECT: research and development project from 1942-1946 that created the first atomic bombs
- SUITCASE NUKE: portable atomic bomb usually transported by suitcase (or other method) to conceal it

3245.98 ● ● ●

CHAPTER THREE

IN PLAY

1324.014

"That would make the rest of you Shadow Squadron, I presume," Howard continued before anyone could reply. He scanned the soldiers' faces until he found Lancaster. "And that would make you Lancaster. You're the one that shot my old boss. You do *not* have a lot of friends in the SAD right now."

Lancaster elected not to reply.

"You've got to admit," Shepherd said in her defence. "He had it coming."

"And me, fellas?" Howard asked, looking back to Cross. "What have I got coming? What has brought the fabled Shadow Squadron all the way out here? Is it bullets? It's bullets, isn't it?"

"You're wanted for questioning regarding your involvement with Bradley Upton's crimes," Cross answered. He didn't owe Howard an answer. In fact, Cross could have just ordered Williams to knock him out and carry him away like a sack of potatoes.

But Cross had to admit that he was a little impressed with this Carter Howard. It took a special kind of courage to make jokes and remain relaxed with several elite soldiers pointing guns at you.

"Shadow Squadron, Wraith is inbound," the stealth helicopter's pilot reported over Cross's canalphone. "ETA is five minutes."

Howard heaved a theatrical sigh of relief. "Oh, is that all?" he said. "Guys, I'll tell you whatever you want to know about Upton's little scam. If you don't mind me talking quickly, I can give you the whole story. Then we can all go our separate ways in about five minutes."

"That's not an option," Paxton said.

"Listen, Commander Cross," Howard said, ignoring Paxton. "I'm sensitive to your information needs, but I've got a job to do and my time's running out. Now if you're not going to ask me any questions, I'll just sum up what I know as best I can. Up until last year, I worked in a special missions unit in Iraq under Bradley Upton. We did a lot of increasingly shady stuff in the name of stabilizing that country after Saddam fell. However, I was the only one who seemed to have a problem with any of it. None of the others were bothered by what we were getting up to, so I confronted Upton about it. He didn't even try to deny how corrupt he was. He just offered me a piece of the action in return for my silence."

"And you took it," Cross said.

Howard's eyes thinned in seemingly genuine annoyance. "You didn't. Why should I have?"

A frown clouded Cross's face.

"No," Howard went on. "I told him I had no interest in his dirty business. I might have also fibbed just a little bit and told him that I had a lovely stockpile of evidence against him that would immediately see the light of day if anything were to happen to me. So Upton and I shook hands on our little gentlemen's agreement and went our separate ways. I got transferred here to start picking Jundallah apart from the inside. Brad got transferred out to Yemen shortly after that. And that's where his story ended – though you wrote that chapter, so you probably know it better than I do."

"Your superiors say you've gone dark," Cross cut in. Howard had barely taken a breath since his story began. Evidently, he meant to get his whole spiel out before the Wraith arrived. "You've refused reassignment and broken off contact."

"I'm undercover," Howard replied. "I can't exactly call the Home Office every weekend to let everybody know I'm okay. These people trust me well enough, but if they catch me reporting to the CIA, what do you think they'll do to me? Anyway, as for refusing reassignment, all I've done is explain to my supervisors that I haven't finished doing the job they sent me here to do. They understand that."

"They had to send two agents to fetch you," Paxton said. "Was that before or after you gave them your so-called explanation?"

"You don't know what you're talking about," Howard said, his expression suddenly blank.

"We know the men the CIA sent to get you suddenly disappeared," Cross said.

"Yeah, they disappeared," Howard said hotly. "Because they're dead."

Cross cocked an eyebrow like a police officer who'd just tricked a criminal into admitting he was guilty.

Howard read Cross's expression correctly, but instead of looking defensive, he tilted his head in disappointment. "Commander, those two guys who came for me weren't beloved co-workers trying to give me first-class tickets back home to the Company Christmas party," he said. "They were Bradley Upton's thugs. I was in the shower one night when they kicked in my bedroom door and opened fire."

To illustrate his point, Howard mimed pulling triggers with both hands. He didn't explain how he managed to escape that particular situation or how the other two men had ended up dead.

"And okay, after that I suppose you could say I went dark," Carter continued. "But it's not because I'm following Brad's example. It's because even though Brad's dead, somebody believes my little story about having a pile of evidence against him. And that somebody doesn't want whatever they think I know getting out to bite them. I've got to tell you, that makes me wish I really did have a pile of evidence to protect myself. I mean … the terrible things we sometimes have to do in the SAD are supposed to be a burden and a responsibility, not a way to make ourselves rich. Upton forgot that fact, and he paid the price. I'd rather not pay that price, too, just so someone higher-up than Upton can pretend none of it ever happened."

Howard paused again, and it wasn't just to catch his breath. Cross noted Carter's jaw muscles were bunched as he scowled at the ground. A little shiver of tension went through Carter as bitter frustration passed over his face. Cross realized what the SAD operative was talking about truly upset him. It upset him so much, it seemed, that he'd said more than he had intended and had to regain his composure.

"Tell me this," Cross said. "Why are you still here? Why not run or disappear when people came gunning for you?"

"You CIA guys are supposed to be pretty good at that," Jannati added.

Howard took a deep breath. He straightened his shoulders and sat up straight once more. He hadn't yet risen from where he sat in the van. "I stayed," he said, "because the job's not done. And because I'm not the sort of person who leaves things unfinished, even if two men try to kill me while I'm wearing nothing but a bath towel."

Shepherd sniggered. "I think I like this guy," he whispered to Williams.

"So what is the job, exactly?" Cross asked. He'd been peering intently at Howard the whole time, absorbing every detail of the man's story and his behaviour. As the CIA agent spoke, Cross weighed up the information he was getting from him against what he already knew about him from studying his history, his Army service record and his CIA dossier.

"Jundallah's trying to build a nuclear bomb," Howard replied. "And I have to do everything I can to stop them."

Howard had been expecting a shocked gasp or total surprise from Cross, but all he got in response was, "Explain."

"Okay..." the rogue CIA agent said, deflated by the fact that his dramatic punchline had failed to land. "Back in 2011, Mossad sent a team here to disrupt Iran's nuclear programme. They funded and trained a local dissident group called the People's Mujahedin to do the dirty work. Before Iran caught on, the PM had killed five prominent nuclear scientists. Well, one of the scientists who survived is the one we're worried about now. His name's Aryo Barzan. He was a professor at the Iran University of Science and Technology. He was instrumental in the completion of the Bushehr Nuclear Power Plant. My info on him suggests he's one of those pure science types, like Oppenheimer, who doesn't care what his science is used for because he's too busy unravelling the mysteries of the universe to think about the dangers."

Lancaster flinched. "Oppenheimer spent decades after the Manhattan Project arguing against nuclear proliferation."

"Also, Barzan's broke and Jundallah's got money," Howard said.

Lancaster frowned.

"Anyway, Barzan went underground with the help of a cousin who is a lieutenant under the supplier we sell our opium to. The cousin contacted us recently on Barzan's behalf, extending an offer to build us a bomb if we could make it worth Barzan's while. The first thing we're supposed to do is get a shipment of opium to Barzan's cousin without his boss knowing about it, so he can branch out on his own. Doing that buys us our first face-to-face meeting with Barzan."

"Do you think the cousin is honest?" Cross asked.

"Hard to say," Howard admitted. "He's a weasel, and he doesn't like his boss very much. Wanting some opium of his own fits his character. He's definitely Aryo Barzan's cousin, that much checks out. Whether he's actually in contact with Barzan and is working to set up a real meeting, I can't say. He could just be stringing us along, seeing how much money he can get out of us. Or he could be part of a sting set up by the Iranian government. I don't know. That's what I'm trying to work out."

Howard paused for dramatic effect. "But if there really is a cobbled-together suitcase nuke in play," he said, "I'm not about to let a load of terrorists get their hands on it."

"Fair point," Cross said. "In that case, how would you feel about having a little backup?"

INTEL

DECRYPTING

12345

COM CHATTER

- EXTRACT: remove to safety

- OP: short for operation, which is a mission

- OPIUM: drug made from the dried, condensed juice of a poppy plant

- GPS TRANSPONDER: device used to locate people or things by way of a Global Positioning System

3245.98 ● ● ●

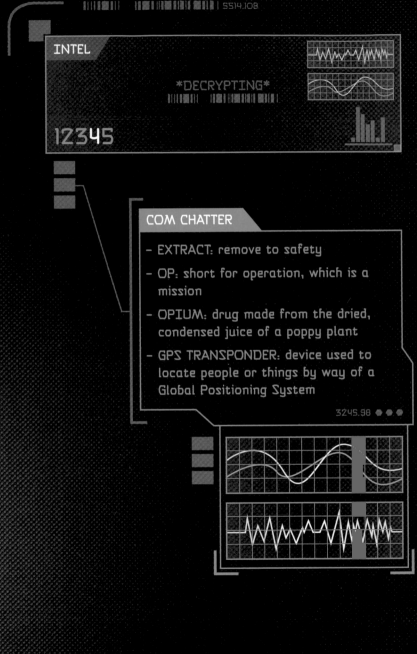

CHAPTER FOUR

BACKUP

It was hard to say who was more surprised by Cross's offer – Carter Howard or the other members of Shadow Squadron.

Howard responded first. "Um, what?"

Paxton found his words next. "Sir?"

"The way I see it," Cross replied, "my team's a soldier down, and you're running a solo op in unfriendly territory without support. You want to get this job done. I still want to pick your brains about Upton's operation. So let's help each other out. We'll see you through to the end of your op and then extract you. In return, you come back with us and tell us what we need to know. What do you think?"

Howard gave a shrug that was supposed to look casual but betrayed his relief. "That beats getting gunned down in the shower," he joked. "But this is my op. We run it my way."

"No," Cross said.

"Then I want her phone number," Howard said, glancing at Lancaster.

"Absolutely not," Lancaster said.

"No," Cross said at the same time.

"Is that your stealth helicopter I see zooming in over the hill there?" Carter asked.

"It is," Cross said.

"I want to fly it," Carter said.

"That we can do," Cross said.

Howard blinked. "Really?" he asked.

"No," Cross said.

Howard sighed.

* * *

Howard set the proceedings in motion with a call to the second-in-command of his Jundallah cell. That man, the younger brother of the cell's actual leader, who was slain in the shoot-out with the Pakistanis, had remained behind at the cell's base of operations to keep an eye on the group's weapons and ammunition. Howard knew him to be a timid man who preferred to hide in his older brother's shadow.

The fake panic in Howard's voice drummed up real panic in the new leader, just as he'd hoped it would. He kept the man focussed on his story with a wild and terrifying tale of ambush and betrayal at the hands of the Al-Qaeda opium smugglers.

Howard even acted out the sounds of whizzing bullets, thundering grenades and screaming Pakistanis as he spoke.

The knockout blow came when he told the Iranian that his brother had been the first to die in the ambush. He and the others had stood their ground to defend his brother's honour, but only he and one other man had survived the battle.

(The last detail about there being a second survivor was Cross's idea. There was no way that Cross would let Carter go alone to meet this man, even if he did feel confident he was telling the truth about everything.)

The new cell leader was so shaken and distraught by Howard's story that he broke down into tortured sobs. Howard winced at that, but he had to press his advantage while he still could. He asked if maybe he should call some members of the other local cells to come and collect the oil tankers and stash them somewhere. The leader agreed without thinking about it. Howard mentioned that the Pakistanis had fled when their own casualties had piled up, leaving their opium behind.

In his blind grief, the new "leader" didn't think to ask why the Pakistanis would bring their opium with them if the attack had been a planned betrayal all along. In fact, the leader didn't say anything at all until Howard prompted him. He asked if he and the other survivor should go ahead with the meeting with Barzan's cousin, which was scheduled for that night.

The leader sobbed a "Yes" in response and told Howard to carry on with the plan. Howard gave Cross a thumbs-up. He stayed on the phone a little longer, giving the crying man some insincere condolences about his older brother's death. In a last-second moment of inspiration, he vowed that the dead cell leader and all those who had fallen with him would be avenged. As soon as he said it, he hung up, hoping to plant a seed of bitter mistrust that might grow and flourish into full-bloom animosity between Jundallah and Al-Qaeda one day. It was a longshot, but one Howard seemed to feel was worth trying.

Meanwhile, Jannati and Williams stripped off one of the dead terrorist's clothes and equipment. When Jannati had changed into the man's clothes, he appeared to have been wounded in the shoulder but otherwise unhurt. He hid most of his face in cloth. Howard remarked that he looked the part well enough to accompany him on the meet.

"Yassir's been around before, when we've dealt with the Persian Knights," Howard said of the dead man when Jannati had finished putting on his clothes. "But Arash – that's Doctor Barzan's cousin, by the way – never paid him any attention. If I can keep his attention, he'll never know the real deal's been replaced with fool's gold."

"Replaced with what?" Jannati asked, unsure if he'd just been insulted.

Howard sighed. "No offence." He turned to Cross, who was closer to him in age than Jannati was. "These kids are so sensitive these days, aren't they?"

"Just call the doctor's cousin and set up the meeting," Paxton said.

While Howard did so, Lancaster dug a pair of small GPS transponders out of a box of gadgets and brought one to Jannati. He exchanged his bracer and tactical datapad for it.

"It's got a panic button if you can't talk over the canalphone," she told him. She gave the second transponder to Howard and helped him hide it.

"Listen up," Cross told Jannati when Lancaster was helping Howard. "Do not let Howard out of your sight. I believe his story, but don't take any chances. Stick to him like glue. If he gives you any reason to think he's not on the level, take him down. I'd rather have him alive, but use your judgement."

"Sir," Jannati said.

"We'll be in earshot," Cross finished. "Call us if you need us."

Jannati nodded then went over to Howard, who had just finished conferring with Lancaster about the logistics of the mission.

"Arash will be looking for us at midday at the run-down garage he owns," Howard told Cross.

"Where?" Cross asked.

"I've got it, Sir," Lancaster said, raising her forearm so he could see the map on her tactical datapad.

"And the other Barzan will be there?" Paxton asked. "The nuclear scientist one?"

"Aryo," Howard said. "And no. We're just dropping the opium truck off there. Arash, the cousin, will take us out to wherever he's got Aryo hidden. He didn't say where that was, though."

"Here's the play," Cross said. "Agent Howard, you'll take Lieutenant Jannati to the garage, drop off the opium, and try to get Barzan to tell you his cousin's location. Lancaster and I will follow you in the Pakistanis' pick-up. The rest of you will stay with the Wraith and park it somewhere hidden, but be ready to jump when we know where the doctor is. We'll coordinate the specifics on the way."

"Sir," his soldiers answered.

Yamashita, Shepherd, Williams and Paxton headed for the Wraith. Lancaster went to the Pakistanis' abandoned pick-up to get it started. Yamashita and Howard began walking towards the box truck full of Pakistani opium.

When Jannati was just out of earshot, Cross caught Howard by the elbow and leaned close to speak quietly to him. "Listen–" he began.

"I know, I know, Commander," Howard cut in. "I'll have your lieutenant back by dusk, freshly waxed, and with a full tank of gas. Not a scratch on him."

"I'll hold you to that," Cross said, amused despite himself. He released Howard's arm. "All right, get going. We'll be watching."

INTEL

DECRYPTING

12345

COM CHATTER

- AK-47: inexpensive assault rifle
- DESERT EAGLE .50: powerful semi-automatic pistol
- EVAC: short for evacuation
- FOUR-EYES: custom unmanned aerial drone (UAV) created by former Shadow Squadron member Edgar Brighton

3245.98 ● ● ●

BLUFFING

The first part of the impromptu mission went perfectly. The Wraith pilot found an abandoned limestone quarry to hide the helicopter in. Cross and Lancaster were able to follow Jannati and Howard's box truck unseen and without incident. They parked around the corner from the garage Arash Barzan owned, and Lancaster was able to launch Four-Eyes and perch it near by where no one on the street could see it.

To their surprise, the gangster wasn't there when they arrived. Howard called him, and the gangster complained of traffic and begged them to wait.

Howard played cagey and paranoid but agreed to wait with the truck until Arash arrived.

While they waited, Lancaster turned to Cross. "Question for you, Sir," she said.

"Let me guess: why do I trust Howard?" he asked.

"I assume you have your reasons, but … yes, Sir. Why?" she asked.

"Let me ask you something first," Cross said. "Do the others ever invite you to play poker with them?"

Lancaster raised an eyebrow. "I went a couple of times," she said. "They haven't played since Yemen."

"Did they happen to tell you why they stopped inviting me?" Cross asked.

"Not in so many words," Lancaster said. "They implied that you won too much."

"Yep," Cross said proudly. "Some of it's luck, sure. But for the most part, playing poker is about reading people. And I'm the best at reading people. No matter how well I know somebody, I can always tell when they're playing straight with me and when

they're lying through their teeth. Agent Howard's not lying."

"I see," Lancaster said thoughtfully. "But what if your instincts are—"

"Car coming," Cross interrupted. He pointed at the laptop screen on Lancaster's knees, showing what Four-Eyes was seeing.

A nondescript black vehicle was pulling up to the garage where Howard and Jannati waited. A balding man in a Western suit and overpriced sunglasses got out, the afternoon sun glaring on a pair of thick gold chains around his neck. Cross assumed the man was Arash Barzan. Howard confirmed the assumption by embracing the newcomer and seeming very relieved to see him. Jannati stayed by the car, putting on his best impression of someone rattled and half in shock from the morning's gunfight.

"Somebody else is in the car," Lancaster said.

Cross hunched over to peer at Lancaster's laptop screen. "Maybe it's the doctor," he said, watching the scene.

"I can't tell," Lancaster said.

"I don't suppose you speak Persian?" Cross asked.

Through Four-Eyes' microphone, they could hear the conversation between Howard and the newly arrived Arash Barzan. However, neither of them could understand it well enough to follow it. Having to ask the question sent a pang through Cross. Not for the first time, he missed his former second-in-command, Chief Walker. Walker spoke more languages than everyone else on the team put together, and each one as fluently as a native. Tragically, he'd suffered career-ending injuries in a bomb blast in Yemen.

"My laptop's got a voice-to-text translator," Lancaster said. "But the live feed from Four-Eyes is lagging. I'm only just getting, 'I'll see you soon,' from the phone call."

Cross frowned. "As soon as Howard gets Barzan to tell him where he's got his cousin stashed, I want you to pinpoint it on the map. Whatever you have to do. Hacking, cracking, web … crawling. Whatever is best."

Lancaster smirked and said, "Yes, Sir."

BLEEP!

"Wait. Something's happening," Lancaster said. She turned the laptop towards Cross so he could see the screen.

Glancing back and forth between the screen and the actual scene down the road, Cross saw Arash Barzan step away from Howard, after a few minutes of close conversation, and gesture towards the car he'd arrived in. Howard had stiffened, and he was signalling behind his back to get Jannati's attention. Jannati was looking from Howard to the car tensely. As the two men watched, Arash opened the passenger door of his car to let the second man out.

"Wait – maybe that is the doctor," Lancaster said. "But I thought they were meeting elsewhere."

The second man stepped out of the car. Suddenly, Howard lurched sideways and dove into Jannati, tackling him to the ground. The two of them rolled under the box truck they'd arrived in and disappeared from sight.

BANG!

The crack of a gunshot shattered the afternoon stillness, sending pigeons flying and awakening shouts from inside the warehouse. Cross realized that the gunshot had come from Arash Barzan. He'd yanked a nickel-plated Desert Eagle .50 from a holster under his jacket and was spraying bullets into the wall and then the ground at Howard and Jannati.

Reacting a mere moment behind Barzan, the second man who'd arrived with him produced an AK-47 rifle from inside the car and aimed into the garage.

"Out!" Cross snapped, opening the pick-up door and yanking his M4 out from behind the bench seat. When Lancaster was clear with her own weapon and behind the cover of the nearest building's corner, Cross hit the truck's horn in a long shrill blast then dropped down flat on his stomach beside the vehicle.

The man with the AK-47 turned away from Howard and Jannati and took aim at the unexpected sound.

BANG BANG BANG BANG!

He squeezed off a long, surprised burst of fire. The shots were wild and missed the truck altogether. Cross's shot, however, was right on the mark.

POP!

From his prone shooting position, Cross shot the man in the chest. He dropped in a heap on the ground, and his AK-47 clattered away into the gutter.

Arash Barzan wasn't quite as nervous as his passenger had been. When he heard Cross's horn, he'd dropped to a knee behind his car. He could still see into the garage but had the entire length of his vehicle between himself and the unknown threat Cross represented.

BOOM!
BOOM!

Barzan took a couple of shots towards Howard and Jannati.

POP-POP-POP-POP!

Suppressing fire from Cross's M4 forced Arash back.

"Lieutenant, talk to me," Cross said to Jannati in between shots.

"Howard caught one in the leg," Jannati replied. "We're in the pit under the truck, but our weapons are up top. There's one guy still up behind that car. He's got his phone out. Looks like he's texting somebody."

Cross cursed. "All right, give us a minute. Out." He switched channels on the canalphone and called the Wraith pilot. At the same time, he silently signalled for Lancaster to get moving down the block and around the corner. She nodded and hurried away. "Change of plan," Cross told the pilot. "We need you."

"Fire support or evac?" the pilot asked.

"Evac," Cross replied. A second later, he had to fire another shot at Barzan as the gangster moved to grab his fallen comrade's AK-47.

"Two minutes," the pilot said. "Out."

Fortunately, two minutes was all it took. When Lancaster was out of sight around the corner, Cross popped up into a crouch and moved diagonally into the nearest bit of cover he could find.

POP!

POP!

He squeezed off two more shots to keep Barzan pinned down. The gangster stuck his Desert Eagle over the boot of the car and fired blindly. Except for a ricochet that buzzed past Cross's ear, none of the shots were anywhere close. Cross took a breath, calmed himself, then burst out of cover again to move forward, squeezing off a little more suppressing fire along the way.

BOOM!

BOOM!

Barzan fired around the side of the car this time and managed to dig up a chunk of pavement between Cross's feet, but that bullet was the last in the clip. When Cross heard the hand cannon's magazine slide free, he charged across the last bit of distance and took cover on the opposite side of the car.

CLACK! CLICK!

Barzan slammed a fresh magazine in place and racked a bullet into the chamber. But what he didn't realize was that Cross's approach was just a feint to keep him distracted. As the gangster stood to take aim at Cross, Lancaster popped out from an alley behind him. She shouted a warning, but rather than stop and surrender, Barzan turned his gun on her and fired.

BOOM!

His shot hit Lancaster just below the shoulder, but she managed to keep hold of her rifle.

POP-POP-POP!

Lancaster nailed Barzan with a three-round burst. The gangster spun and collapsed on top of the car and slid onto the pavement. Cross kicked the gun out of his hand. Barzan sighed, lay on his back, and coughed up blood.

"Sergeant?" Cross called over to Lancaster.

"Bullet just took some meat with it," Lancaster said. She walked over to Cross with one hand clamped down over her wounded shoulder. Her voice was low, and she was steady on her feet, but her skin was pale. "I'll be all right."

Howard and Jannati emerged from the garage, Howard leaning heavily on Jannati with Jannati's wrap tied around Howard's bleeding thigh.

"Pretty sure I'm dying, if anybody's interested," Howard said. Except for a grimace of pain, however, he looked better off than Lancaster did.

"Ask him where his cousin is," Cross said to Howard, glancing down at Arash Barzan.

The gangster was still alive, but only just. Howard asked him where his cousin was, which earnt him a raspy reply from Barzan followed by a hoarse, gurgling laugh. The laugh turned into a cough, which tapered off into an eerie rattle. Then he died.

"Of course you did, you slick rat," Howard said softly when Barzan was dead. Through his pain, a faint smirk was just visible.

"Well?" Cross asked.

"He said he gave his cousin up to the People's Mujahedin in 2012," Howard said. "He used the money they gave him to buy the guns he was going to use to overthrow his boss in the Persian Knights. He was going to use this opium to flood the market and undercut his old boss's prices. I suppose he was planning to drive us out somewhere secret to 'meet his cousin' and put a couple of bullets in our heads. That must've been the original plan, anyway."

Jannati helped Howard sit on the hood of the gangster's car then moved to help Cross get a bandage around Lancaster's shoulder.

"What changed?" Cross said. "What happened over here?"

"I miscounted," Howard said with a sneer of disappointment. He looked over at the man Cross had shot. "See that guy? He was part of my cell. He went with us to meet the Pakistanis. He got away during your little ambush, but I didn't realize. Evidently, he came back afterwards and saw us all talking and making our little plans. After that, he must've called Arash directly to tell him I was a traitor. As soon as I realized that's who Arash had in the car, I knew we were blown."

Howard paused and looked at Jannati. "Sorry about your ribs, by the way," Howard said. "Didn't really have time to explain everything in the heat of the moment."

"Plus," Jannati grunted, "if the Commander had seen you just dive for cover without a word and leave me standing there to get shot to pieces, he might have jumped to the wrong conclusion, you know?"

Howard laughed, then winced as a jolt of pain went through his wounded leg. "Jannati's a sharp kid," he said.

When the Wraith was a mere couple of blocks away, Cross finally detected the quiet whine of the helicopter's rotors. He tapped his canalphone and told Williams to have his medical kit ready to treat the wounded. Williams acknowledged just as the Wraith set down in the garage's deserted car park.

Yamashita, Paxton, Shepherd and Williams jumped out of the Wraith and hurried over to help the others inside.

"What's your plan now?" Cross asked Howard, slipping an arm under his shoulder to help him hobble to the helicopter. "Your credibility's blown with Jundallah now."

"That it is," Howard said. "I don't suppose you know of any cushy desk jobs in Belize, perhaps?"

Cross chuckled. "Sorry, no," he said. "But I do have a slightly less attractive offer for you. Like I said before, my team's a man down, and the JSOC hasn't been very forthcoming with a replacement."

"Is that a fact?" Howard said. "Can you make that happen?"

"Maybe," Cross said. "I'll have to pull some strings and scratch some backs, but it's not outside the realm of possibility."

Howard dropped his guard. "Interesting," he said warmly. "I'll think about it."

"Take all the time you need," Cross said. "It's a long trip home."

MISSION DEBRIEFING

OPERATION

DRAGON TEETH
010

PRIMARY OBJECTIVES

- Locate Carter Howard

- Question him

STATUS

3/3 COMPLETE

SECONDARY OBJECTIVES

- Destabilize relationship between
  Al-Qaeda and Jundallah

3245.98 ● ● ●

CROSS, RYAN

RANK: Lieutenant Commander
BRANCH: Navy SEAL
PSYCH PROFILE: Team leader
of Shadow Squadron. Control
oriented and loyal, Cross insisted
on hand-picking each member of
his squad.

Well done, soldiers. Lancaster's autoguns performed admirably, and Carter Howard's quick-thinking and selflessness might've saved the life of one of our own.

Yeah, we took a few bullets in the process, but everyone's recovering well. Considering the circumstances, we should all be pleased with the outcome: success and a new team member we can trust.

- Lieutenant Commander Ryan Cross

ERROR
UNAUTHORIZED
USER MUST HAVE LEVEL 12 CLEARANCE
OR HIGHER IN ORDER TO GAIN ACCESS
TO FURTHER MISSION INFORMATION.

2019.681

CLASSIFIED

CREATOR BIO(S)

AUTHOR

CARL BOWEN

Carl Bowen is a father, husband, and writer living in Georgia, USA. He was born in Louisiana, lived briefly in England and was brought-up in Georgia where he went to school. He has published a handful of novels, short stories and comics, including retellings of *20,000 Leagues Under the Sea*, *The Strange Case of Dr. Jekyll and Mr. Hyde*, *The Jungle Book*, *Aladdin and the Magic Lamp*, *Julius Caesar* and *The Murders in the Rue Morgue*. He is the original author of *BMX Breakthrough* as well as the Shadow Squadron series.

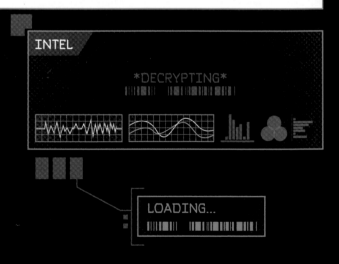

INTEL

DECRYPTING

LOADING...

WILSON TORTOSA

Wilson "Wunan" Tortosa is a Filipino comic book artist best known for his work on *Tomb Raider* and the American relaunch of *Battle of the Planets* for Top Cow Productions. Wilson attended Philippine Cultural High School, then went on to the University of Santo Tomas where he graduated with a degree in Fine Arts.

BENNY FUENTES

Benny Fuentes lives in Tabasco, Mexico, where the temperature is just as hot as the sauce. He studied graphic design in college, but now he works as a full-time illustrator in the comic book and graphic novel industry for companies like Marvel, DC Comics and Top Cow Productions. He shares his home with two crazy cats, Chelo and Kitty, who act like they own the place.

2019.681

AUTHOR DEBRIEFING

CARL BOWEN

Q/When and why did you decide to become a writer?

A/I've enjoyed writing ever since I was at primary school. I wrote as much as I could, hoping to become the next Lloyd Alexander or Stephen King, but I didn't sell my first story until I was at university. It had been a long wait, but the day I saw my story in print was one of the best days of my life.

Q/What made you decide to write *Shadow Squadron*?

A/As a child, my heroes were always brave knights or noble loners who fought because it was their duty, not for fame or glory. I think the special ops soldiers of the US military embody those ideals. Their jobs are difficult and often thankless, so I wanted to show how cool their jobs are and also express my gratitude for our brave warriors.

Q/What inspires you to write?

A/My biggest inspiration is my family. My wife's love and support lifts me up when this job seems too hard to keep going. My son is another big inspiration.

He's three years old, and I want him to read my books and feel the same way I did when I read my favourite books as a child. And if he happens to grow up to become an elite soldier in the US military, that would be pretty awesome, too.

Q/Describe what it was like to write these books.
A/The only military experience I have is a year I spent in the Army ROTC. It gave me a great respect for the military and its soldiers, but I quickly realized I would have made an awful soldier. I recently got to test out firearms for research on this book. I got to blow apart an old fax machine.

Q/What is your favourite book, film and game?
A/My favourite book of all time is *Don Quixote*. It's crazy and it makes me laugh. My favourite film is either *Casablanca* or *Double Indemnity*, old black-and-white films made before I was born. My favourite game, hands down, is *Skyrim*, in which you play a heroic dragonslayer. But not even *Skyrim* can keep me from writing more *Shadow Squadron* stories, so you won't have to wait long to read more about Ryan Cross and his team. That's a promise.

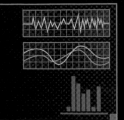

INTEL

DECRYPTING

ALPHA

COM CHATTER

-MISSION PREVIEW: After an unknown aircraft crashes in Antarctica near a science facility, Shadow Squadron is deployed to recover the device. But when Russian special forces intervene, Cross gets caught between the mission's objective and the civilian scientists' safety.

3245.98 ● ● ●

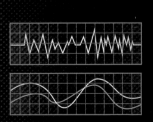

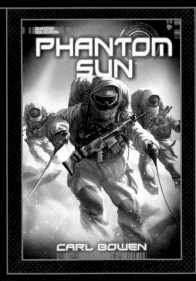

SHADOW SQUADRON

PHANTOM SUN

CARL BOWEN

PHANTOM SUN

Cross tapped his touch screen to start the video. On the screen, a few geologists began pointing and waving frantically. The camera watched them all for another couple of seconds then lurched around in a semicircle and tilted skywards. Blurry clouds wavered in and out of focus for a second before the cameraman found what the others had been pointing at – a lance of white fire in the sky. The image focused, showing what appeared to be a meteorite with a trailing white plume behind it punching through a hole in the clouds. The camera zoomed out to allow the cameraman to better track the object's progress through the sky.

"Is that a meteorite?" Shepherd asked.

"Just keep watching," Brighton said, breathless with anticipation.

Right on cue, the supposed meteorite suddenly flared white, then changed direction in mid-flight by almost 45 degrees. Grunts and hisses of surprise filled the room.

"So ... not a meteorite," Shepherd muttered.

The members of Shadow Squadron watched as the falling object changed direction once again with another flare and then pitched downwards. The camera angle twisted overhead and then lowered to track its earthward trajectory from below.

"And now ... sonic boom," Brighton said.

The camera image shook violently for a second as the compression wave from the falling object broke the speed of sound and as the accompanying burst shook the cameraman's hands. A moment later, the object streaked into the distance and disappeared into the rolling hills of ice and snow. The video footage ended a few moments later with a still image of the

gawking geologists looking as excited as children on Christmas morning.

"This video popped up on the internet a few hours ago," Cross began. "It's already started to go viral."

"What is it?" Second Lieutenant Aram Jannati said. Jannati, the team's newest member, came from the Marine Special Operations Regiment. "I can't imagine we'd get involved if it was just a meteor."

"Meteorite," Staff Sergeant Adam Paxton corrected. "If it gets through the atmosphere to the ground, it's a meteorite."

"That wasn't a meteorite, man," Brighton said, hopping out of his chair. He dug his smartphone out of a pocket and walked around the table towards the front of the room. He laid his phone on the touch screen Cross had used, and then synced up the two devices. With that done, he used his phone as a remote control to run the video backwards to the first time the object had changed directions. He used a slider to move the timer back and forth, showing the object's fairly sharp angle of deflection through the sky.

"Meteorites can't change direction like this," Brighton said. "This is 45 degrees of deflection at least, and it barely even slows down."

"I'm seeing a flare when it turns," Paxton said. "Meteors hold a lot of frozen water when they're in space. It expands when it reaches the atmosphere. If those gases are venting or exploding, couldn't that cause a change of direction?"

"Not this sharply," Brighton said before Cross could reply. "Besides, if you look at this..." He used a few swipes across his phone to pause the video and zoom in on the flying object. At the new resolution, a dark, oblong shape was visible inside a wreath of fire. He then advanced through the first and second changes of direction and tracked it a few seconds forward before pausing again. "See?"

A room full of shrugs and uncomprehending looks met Brighton's eager gaze.

"It's the same size!" Brighton said, throwing his hands up in mock frustration. "If this thing had exploded twice – and with enough force to push something this big in a different direction both times – it would be in a million pieces. So those aren't explosions. They're thrusters or something."

"Which makes this what?" Shepherd asked. "A UFO?"

"Sure," Paxton answered in a mocking tone. "It's unidentified, it's flying and it's surely an object. It probably has little green men inside, too."

"You don't know that it doesn't," Brighton said. "I mean, it could be from outer space!"

"Sit down, Sergeant," Chief Walker said.

Brighton reluctantly did so, pocketing his phone.

"Don't get ahead of yourself, Ed," Cross said, retaking control of the briefing. "Phantom Cell analysts have authenticated the video and concluded that this thing isn't just a meteorite. It's some sort of metal construct, though they can't make out specifics from the quality of the video. I suppose it's possible it's from outer space, but it's much more likely to be man-made. All we know for certain is that it's not American made. Therefore, our mission is to get out to where it came down, secure it, zip it up and bring it back for a full analysis. Any questions so far?"

"I have one," Jannati said. "What is Phantom Cell?"

Cross nodded. Jannati was the newest member of the team, and as such he wasn't as familiar with all the various secret programmes. "Phantom Cell is a parallel programme to ours," Cross explained. "But their focus is on psy-ops, cyberwarfare and research and development."

Jannati nodded. "Geeks, in other words," he said. Brighton gave him a sour look but said nothing.

"What are we supposed to do about the scientists who found this thing?" Lieutenant Kimiyo Yamashita asked. True to his stoic nature, the sniper had finished his breakfast and coffee while everyone else was talking excitedly. "Do they know we're coming?"

"That's the problem," Cross said, frowning. "We haven't heard a peep out of them since this video appeared online. Attempts to contact them have gone unanswered. The last anyone heard, the geologists who made the video were going to try to find the point of impact where this object came down. We have no idea whether they found it or not, or what happened to them."

"Isn't this how the film *Aliens* started?" Brighton asked. "With a space colony suddenly cutting off communication after a UFO crash landing?"

Paxton rolled his eyes. "Lost Aspen, the base there, is pretty new," he said. "And it's in the middle of Antarctica. It could just be a simple technical failure."

"You have no imagination, man," Brighton said. "You're going to be the first one the monster eats. Well … after me, anyway."

"These are our orders," Cross continued as if he hadn't been interrupted. "Find what crashed, bring the object back for study, work out why the research station stopped communicating and make sure the civilians are safe. Stealth is going to be of paramount importance here. Nobody has any territorial claims on Marie Byrd Land, but no country is supposed to be sending troops on missions anywhere in Antarctica, either."

"Are we expecting anyone else to be breaking that rule while we are, Commander?" Yamashita asked.

"It's possible," Cross said. "If this object is man-made, whoever made it is probably going to come looking for it. Any other government that attached the same significance to the video that ours did could send people, too. No specific intel has been confirmed yet, but it's only a matter of time before someone takes an active interest."

"Seems like the longer the video's out there, the more likely we're going to have company," Yamashita said.

"About that," Cross said with a mischievous smile on his face. "Phantom Cell's running a psy-ops campaign in support of our efforts. They're simultaneously spreading the word that the video's a hoax and doing their best to stop it from spreading and to remove it from circulation."

"Good luck to them on that last one," Brighton snorted. "It's the internet. Phantom Cell's good, but nobody's that good."

"Not our concern," Cross said. "We ship out in one hour. Get your equipment onto the Commando. We'll go over more mission specifics during the flight. Understood?"

"Sir," the men responded in unison. At a nod from Cross, they rose and gathered up the remains of their breakfast. As they left the briefing room, Walker remained behind. He gulped down the last of his coffee before standing up.

"Brighton's certainly excited," Walker said.

"I knew he would be," Cross replied. "I didn't expect him to try to help out so much with the briefing, though."

"Is that what I'm like whenever I chip in from up here?" Walker asked.

Cross fought off the immediate urge to toy with his second-in-command, though he couldn't stop the mischievous smile from coming back. "Maybe a little bit," he said.

Walker returned Cross's grin. "Then I wholeheartedly apologize."

TRANSMISSION ERROR

PLEASE CONTACT YOUR LOCAL LIBRARY OR
BOOKSELLER FOR MORE DETAILS...

SEA DEMON
CARL BOWEN

BLACK ANCHOR
CARL BOWEN

EAGLE DOWN
CARL BOWE

SNIPER SHIELD
CARL BOWEN

WHITE NEEDLE
CARL BOWEN

PHANTOM SUN
CARL BOWEN

SAND SPIDER
CARL BOWEN

DARK AGENT
CARL BOWEN

GUARDIAN ANGEL
CARL BOWEN

DRAGON TEETH
CARL BOWEN

LONG SHADOW
CARL BOWEN

STEEL HAMMER
CARL BOWEN

2012.101